The SWEETEST WITCH Around

Alison McGHEE   Harry BLISS

A PAULA WISEMAN BOOK

Simon & Schuster Books for Young Readers

New York London Toronto Sydney New Delhi

SIMON & SCHUSTER BOOKS FOR YOUNG READERS
An imprint of Simon & Schuster Children's Publishing Division
1230 Avenue of the Americas, New York, New York 10020
Text copyright © 2014 by Alison McGhee
Illustrations copyright © 2014 by Harry Bliss
SIMON & SCHUSTER BOOKS FOR YOUNG READERS is a trademark of Simon & Schuster, Inc.
For information about special discounts for bulk purchases, please contact Simon & Schuster
Special Sales at 1-866-506-1949 or business@simonandschuster.com.
The Simon & Schuster Speakers Bureau can bring authors to your live event. For more information
or to book an event, contact the Simon & Schuster Speakers Bureau at 1-866-248-3049 or visit our
website at www.simonspeakers.com.
Book design by Lucy Cummins
The text for this book is set in Aunt Mildred.
The illustrations for this book are rendered in black ink and watercolor
on Arches 90 lb watercolor paper.
Manufactured in China
0514 SCP
2 4 6 8 10 9 7 5 3 1
Library of Congress Cataloging-in-Publication Data
McGhee, Alison, 1960–
The sweetest witch around / Alison McGhee ; illustrated by Harry Bliss.
pages cm
"A Paula Wiseman Book."
Summary: On Halloween, a little witch and her baby sister study humans and their mysterious ways.
ISBN 978-1-4424-7833-6 (hardcover) – ISBN 978-1-4424-7838-1 (ebook)
[1. Witches—Fiction. 2. Sisters—Fiction. 3. Halloween—Fiction.] I. Bliss, Harry, 1964– illustrator.
II. Title.
PZ7.M4784675Sw 2014
[E]—dc23
2013017903

To Evan McGhee and Arthur McGhee,
the sweetest nephews around
—A. M.

For all the kids at the
Singapore American School
—H. B.